I0648920

Mary Jones Stimson Clark, Andrew Bigelow, Manlius Stimson
Clarke

Memorial of Reverend Pitt Clarke

Pastor of the First Congregational Church in Norton, Mass. and of Mary

Jones Clarke

Mary Jones Stimson Clark, Andrew Bigelow, Manlius Stimson Clarke

Memorial of Reverend Pitt Clarke
Pastor of the First Congregational Church in Norton, Mass. and of Mary Jones Clarke

ISBN/EAN: 9783337715670

Printed in Europe, USA, Canada, Australia, Japan

Cover: Foto ©Raphael Reischuk / pixelio.de

More available books at **www.hansebooks.com**

MEMORIAL

OF

REV. PITT CLARKE,

PASTOR OF THE

FIRST CONGREGATIONAL CHURCH IN NORTON, MASS.;

AND OF

MARY JONES CLARKE,

(HIS WIFE.)

PRINTED FOR PRIVATE DISTRIBUTION

CAMBRIDGE:

PRESS OF JOHN WILSON AND SON.

1866.

MEMOIR, AUTOBIOGRAPHY,

AND

CONFESSION OF FAITH

OF

REV. PITT CLARKE.

"When Faith and Love, which parted from thee never,
Had ripened thy just soul to dwell with God,
Meekly thou didst resign this earthly load
Of Death, called Life." — *Milton.*

CONTENTS.

Preface to Memoir of Rev. Pitt Clarke

Memoir of Rev. Pitt Clarke . . . .

Autobiography of Rev. Pitt Clarke .

Confession of Faith ; or, A Pastor's Legacy

Preface to Memoir of Mary Jones Clarke

Memoir of Mary Jones Clarke

Poems by Mary Jones Clarke . .

PREFACE.

THE following sketch of the Rev. PITT CLARKE was written by his son, Manlius Stimson Clarke, Esq. It appeared originally in the Rev. S. H. Emery's History of the Ministry of Taunton, a town which formerly included Norton within its corporate limits. Not long after this sketch was written, the author of it joined his father in the world beyond the grave. He was a worthy son of the good and pious man, whose life he had portrayed, and whose Christian virtues he emulated. He died in the prime of life, and in the midst of a most useful and honorable career.

In Mr. Clarke's diary, which is alluded to in the following pages, there is a brief Autobiography. It appears from the date of the Autobiography, that it was written Jan. 15, 1832, the birthday of his seventieth year. Many of the incidents which it relates are, of course, to be found in the Memoir by his son; but its intrinsic value and touching simplicity are such as to render any memorial of Mr. Clarke incomplete, which does not contain it.

The Confession of Faith which follows the Autobiography was found among Mr. Clarke's manuscripts after his decease. It is evident from its perusal, that it was intended for a new-year's gift to his parish. It was afterwards published by his family, and distributed among his parishioners. The exposition which it contains of his views of the Christian faith and the Christian's duty renders it interesting and valuable to all who cherish his memory.

The Confession of Faith, the Autobiography, and the Memoir, are brought together, in this volume, in a more permanent form than they have hitherto received. They possess a peculiar interest for his family. Here they are dedicated to his memory, — to the memory of one who was a loved and revered father, a faithful pastor, and a devout Christian.

EDWARD H. CLARKE.

ARLINGTON STREET. BOSTON.
November, 1866.

MEMOIR

OF

REV. PITT CLARKE.

REV. PITT CLARKE (or Clark, as the name was formerly written), long known as the Pastor of the First Congregational Parish in Norton, Mass., was born at Medfield, in the same State, Jan. 15, 1763. His father, Jacob Clark, was one of three brothers, whose grandfather came from England, and settled in the north of Wrentham. His own grandfather removed to Medfield, and purchased a farm, where some of the descendants of the family still remain. Pitt was one of a family of seven children, for whom the tilling of the soil in a retired New-England village, with constant and severe economy, afforded sufficient but not abundant means of support. In his mother, whose maiden name was Meletiah Hammond, were united an intense religious sensibility, a deep and almost painful feeling of personal responsibility, and a naturally nervous temperament. These all prompted her, early and earnestly, to instil into the minds and hearts of her children a pious reverence towards God, a sense of the great importance of religious interests, and daily habits of devotion, to which, more than to any other outward cause, may be attributed the early determination of this one of her sons to devote himself to the sacred office. An early fondness for the acquisition of knowledge, and a desire to increase his fitness for that high post of duty, led Mr. Clarke to covet eagerly the advantages of a public education. These, however, the straightened circumstances of his family could not readily command, and made it manifest, that, if acquired at all, they must be by his own exertions. Various circumstances conspired to postpone to a comparatively late period any opportunity to accomplish these wishes. His daily services were required upon the farm; public and private interests were disturbed by the War of Independence; he himself was at one time called upon to join the militia of his native town, in a sudden expedition to defend the State against a threatened invasion of the British, by the way of Rhode Island; the destruction of his father's house and furniture by fire (a circumstance of no small moment to a family so situated) all united to frustrate his early endeavors to obtain an education. Soon after the close of the Revolution, however, having by industry and great frugality gathered together a portion of the requisite funds, he applied himself with renewed earnestness to the studies preparatory for entering college. These he pursued by the aid, and under the direction, of the late Hannah Adams, a name widely known in the literature of New England. From her faithful training he passed, with credit, into Harvard University, in July, 1786, at the age of twenty-three years. His mind, naturally vigorous and inquisitive, inclined him more particularly to scientific and classical studies; in these, and especially in the mathematics, his scholarship was sound, and much beyond that usually attained by the graduates of his day.

He received the honors of the University in 1790, but was compelled to devote his first exertions to replenishing the slender capital he had expended for his education, by the emolument of teaching. For two years he took charge of the town school in Cambridge; at the same time, he devoted all the leisure he could command from this duty to the pursuit of his theological studies, and in April, 1792, was examined, and duly approbated to preach, by the Cambridge Association of ministers. After occasional services in neighboring parishes, in August of that year he relinquished his school, and accepted an invitation to preach for the first Congregational society in Norton, whose pulpit had been recently made vacant by the death of the Rev. Joseph Palmer. This was the first place of his preaching as a candidate; and, though the desk had been previously occupied by several others since Mr. Palmer's decease, such was the favor with which his labors were received, that, after preaching only four sabbaths, he received from the church an invitation to become their pastor. This call was sudden and unexpected to him, and, following upon so recent an acquaintance, did not command the unanimous assent of the parish, though seconded by a decided majority in the church. He did not immediately accept it, but, with that cautious judgment for which he was ever distinguished, proposed a temporary arrangement, by which he continued to supply their pulpit during the following winter and spring; thus securing to himself and the parish an opportunity for more mature deliberation, before entering upon an engagement, which was then regarded as terminating only with life. A better acquaintance on the part of the parish served only to increase the confidence his first coming had inspired, and resulted in a renewed and more decided invitation, from church and parish, to make the connection a permanent one. This invitation he accepted, and he was accordingly ordained July 3, 1793, — the services of the occasion being principally performed by the Rev. Thomas Prentiss, of Medfield, who preached the sermon; Rev. Jacob Cushing, of Waltham, who gave the charge: Rev. Roland Green, of Mansfield, who gave the right hand of fellowship.

"A solemn day to me!" says the pastor, in a short autobiographical notice found among his papers after his decease. "My deepest impression was, that I was insufficient for these things. I felt the force of that passage, ' I know not how to

go out or come in before this people,' and made it the subject of my first discourse after ordination."

This, his first field of earthly labor, proved to be the only
one in which he was to work. For two and forty years the
connection thus formed continued unbroken, and was then
broken only by the hand of death. So many years of his
early life, spent by Mr. Clarke in the healthy exercise of the
farm, his constitution of great natural strength and vigor, and
his simple habits of living, to which he always adhered, all
combined to secure to him a life of uninterrupted health and
strength, and enabled him, with a constancy and certainty
rarely equalled, to meet the various and constantly returning
duties of his office. Rarely, if ever, was he known, from any
cause, to be absent from the desk on the sabbath, from the
bedside of the sick and dying, the house of mourning, or any
other station to which duty called, during all the years of
his lengthened ministry. He was remarkable for his habits
of industry, regularity, and order: always an early riser, the
first hours of the morning found him uniformly at his work;
and many of his discourses were prepared during the earliest
hours of days, largely occupied by the labors of the farm.
He continued, during all his life, to supply the deficiencies
of an inadequate salary, by partaking, in common with many
of his parishioners, of the toils of the husbandman, with
which his early training made him familiar.

His whole character, as a man and a minister, was not
only above reproach or question, but was in every respect

faithful and exemplary. Among his clerical brethren he was widely respected for his sound judgment and wise counsel, and was frequently called to assist or preside at their deliberations. He took a hearty and efficient interest in the cause of education, devoting much of his time and attention to the care of the common schools in his parish. He rendered important service, for many years, as a member of the Board of Trustees of the Bristol Academy, in Taunton, and, in 1827, became a life-member of the American Education Society.

He possessed largely the confidence of his people, and his counsel and advice were often sought by them in matters of private and personal concern. Among them he was loved and esteemed, as possessing, in an unusual degree, that quiet evenness of temper, that daily serenity of life, and calmness of judgment, under all circumstances, which must ever form the most trustworthy elements of character. In him, these qualities so constituted the texture of his daily life, that those who knew him best and saw him oftenest, rarely, if ever, saw them in any degree disturbed or shaken.

These characteristics appeared in his public ministrations, and gave to them a quiet and simple earnestness, accompanied by a directness of appeal and application, which rendered them profitable to the people of his charge, and made him an acceptable preacher in all the neighboring pulpits.

Mr. Clarke continued always to enjoy the confidence of the University where he was educated, and his house was often selected by its government as the temporary residence of those whose immediate connection with the College was, from any cause, interrupted; and many passed from his careful hands to the walls of the University.

In the constant but unobtrusive duties of his parish, the forty-two years of his life and his ministry passed away. It appears from the entries in a diary, kept during the last twelve years of his life, and found among his papers after his decease, that a sense of the importance of his duties, and of the obligation to fidelity imposed by his office, deepened as he saw himself approaching the end of his earthly ministry. Though his health and strength failed not, still with each year he seemed more fully to realize that only a few more years remained to him here.

The last entry made in his diary, under date of Jan. 1, 1835, though he was then in perfect health, closes with these words: "The days of my years teach me that the solemn test of my character is at hand; that eternity is at my door; that there is but a step between me and death." This step was shorter even than he anticipated. A short but severe illness, of only eleven days' duration, arrested him in the midst of his active duties, and suffered only a single sabbath to pass between the one which witnessed his last ministrations to his own people and that on which they were summoned to mourn at his funeral. He died Feb. 13, 1835, at the age of seventy-two; meeting the end in a sustained and serene faith, as being but the beginning of the better life. One of

3

his clerical brethren.* who visited him frequently during his sickness, spoke of this dying scene in these words: —

" I testify (and I bless God for the privilege of so testifying), that often as I have stood by the bed of mortal sickness, and prayed and watched and wept as one and another of the spirits of flesh were quitting their tenements of clay, never have I beheld a death-bed scene more sublimely edifying, more Christianly serene, sustained, and consoling, than that of the aged servant of Christ who sleeps in death before us. Truly his latter end was *peace.* He knew in whom he believed, and 'endured, as seeing Him who is invisible.' The Being whom he served, shed down into his soul the gladsome tokens of his presence. Supports he experienced which the world could not give, which flesh and sense were incapable of administering, but which death itself could not take away. 'My heart is fixed,' he exultingly exclaimed, — 'My heart is fixed, trusting, O Lord! in thee. I am now ready to be offered, and the time of my departure is at hand. Father, into thy hands I commend my spirit.' And he sunk from life to rest in peace, and sleep in the 'blessed hope.' "

---

* Rev. Andrew Bigelow, D.D., then minister in Taunton, who preached in Norton on Lord's Day, Feb. 15. 1835, a sermon at the funeral of Mr. Clarke, which was afterwards published.

AUTOBIOGRAPHY

OF

REV. PITT CLARKE.

JAN. 15. — As I have arrived so near threescore years
and ten, — the common age of man, fixed by my Maker,
— I am moved to leave behind me a short memoir of my
life. I dare not neglect it any longer, for fear of death, — I
am so near the boundary of human existence. I am not led
to do this from the impression that any thing in my life will
be worthy of notice, but from a desire to bequeath to my
children a brief memorial of their humble origin.

I was born in Medfield, Jan. 15. 1763. My father's name
was Jacob. He had nothing to recommend him beyond the
reputation of being an honest man, an industrious farmer,
and practical Christian. He was one of three brothers,
whose grandfather came from England, and settled in the
north of Wrentham, which was then comparatively a wilder-

ness. My grandfather came to Medfield, and purchased a farm in the south part of that town by his own industry.

He had three sons and three daughters. He gave his sons the names of Nathan, Jacob, and David, from a kind of veneration for those scriptural characters. They all bore the name of being honest, industrious, and devout. There ever appeared to me to be a perfect harmony and endearing intercourse between them. My mother's name was originally Meletiah Hammant; which, rightly spelt, is Hammond. Her predecessors bore the same reputation with my father. She was my father's second wife.

My mother was of a different texture from my father. He was naturally cheerful and social. She was of a feeble, gloomy, nervous make, and pious almost to superstition. At times, she was so fearful of not living up to that profession of religion which she early made, as to sink almost into despair. This was owing to a great diffidence of herself, united with her nervous affections. She was not only pious in mind, but devout in practice.

She always set a good example before her children, who were three sons and four daughters. She instilled into their minds, when very young, the first principles of religion; and expressed the greatest concern in giving them pious feelings. I feel much indebted to my parents for my early dedication to God in baptism, and my early habits of attention to religious institutions. Especially I feel many obligations to my mother for the many early religious impressions I received from her pious example. I often witnessed, when a small child, her secret prayers; and, when unobserved by her, would sink |down| in the spirit of mental and private devotion. This led me into early habits of calling upon God morning and evening, and of committing to memory a variety of prayers to assist my devotions. This habit of secret prayer never entirely forsook me; though, I acknowledge with shame, I have not always practised it so constantly and fervently as I ought.

My grandfather had an exalted opinion of the great Pitt in his mother country, on account of his distinguished pleas for American liberty. Out of regard to this eloquent friend of America, my grandfather would tell me he gave me my name, and flatter me with the idea of going to college. How far this operated to raise my ambition for study, when a child, I cannot say. I early felt a desire to learn, and was ambitious to excel my classmates. When very young, my master told me I must study the Latin, and go to college. I obtained the consent of my father to begin the first book in Latin when between ten and eleven years old. But I did not continue the study of the language longer than the town-school continued. This was owing to two causes. One was the deranged state of the academies and colleges, on account of the Revolutionary War; the other was the embarrassed condition of my father. In the first of the Revolution, Boston was besieged, and the college entirely broken up. Then there was not the least encouragement of obtaining a public education. I gave up my studies, went to work on the farm

at home, and occasionally abroad on wages; laying aside
what I could against a time of need for an education. When
old enough to be enrolled in the Militia Bill, I was called to
go as a soldier on a sudden expedition to Rhode Island.
The British had taken possession of the island, and were
directing their devastations towards Massachusetts. The
alarm came, and the militia were called upon to meet their
attacks, and drive them from the island. In this expedition,
I was every day expecting to meet the enemy in the hottest
battle; but, just before it came to our turn to fight, the British
were driven from their stronghold, and evacuated the island.
I returned home to my father's farm. As soon as the war
terminated, and the college was restored to its regular state,
I again entertained the hope of resuming my studies. But
another circumstance occurred to disappoint me. My father's
house unfortunately took fire, and was consumed, together
with nearly all the furniture and fall provisions. It was in
November, 1779.

All the little that I had laid aside was destroyed. I felt
myself stript and naked. But from the calamity I learned
some of the best lessons. My father, however, was thrown
into such immediate embarrassment, that I dismissed all
thoughts of pursuing my studies, and was under the necessity of returning to hard labor for a few years. When I
arrived at the age of twenty-one, and felt the liberty of
acting for myself, I resumed the courage of setting out for
an education. I had procured a little to begin with by working at common wages, which my father gave me: and he

promised to assist me some more, if he should be able; though it could be but little. I studied partly at home, and partly with Miss Hannah Adams, who lived near by, and to whom I recited my lessons. Under her tuition principally, I fitted for college, and was admitted into Cambridge University about a year after I commenced my studies, — July 22, 1786.

I had the good fortune of being a member of a large and respectable class, many of whom were of the first talent, and much the greater part of good characters. Another circumstance was much in my favor. The most distinguished scholars in my class were, like myself, in limited circumstances, and the most popular. On this account, the best part of the class set the example of prudence in expenses; and there was no disparagement in it. By receiving help from the charitable funds, and teaching schools, I made my way through college without much assistance from my father. I received the honors of the University, July 21, 1790.

Being in debt for my college expenses, I engaged the town-school in Cambridge, and continued in it two years; at the same time pursuing my theological studies. These studies had been my predilection before I entered college, and were a leading object of attention through my college life. Before I left the school, I was examined by the Cambridge Association of Ministers, and approbated to preach April 17, 1792. I preached occasionally in neighboring towns while I continued in the school; and, before I closed

it, received an application to supply the vacant parish in
Norton. I commenced preaching in this place as soon as I
left the school, — the following August. It was the first
place of my preaching on probation.

Having preached here only four sabbaths, the church in
Norton gave me an invitation to settle among them as their
gospel minister. The invitation was so sudden and unexpected, that I at first felt ready to reject it. It being, however, of such a serious nature, I took it into consideration;
and consented to supply the pulpit myself, or by proxy, till I
gave my answer. I found the people much divided. They
had heard many candidates, and could not unite on any one.
The opposition to me, at first, was formidable. I could not
satisfy the minds of those called orthodox. On this account,
the society postponed their meeting, to concur with the
church, for several months, on condition I would continue to
preach with them longer. It being winter, and bad moving
about, I consented to tarry with them till spring. This gave
us an opportunity to become acquainted with each other;
and, upon this farther acquaintance. the opposition in a great
measure subsided; and there was nearly a unanimous invitation from church and society for me to become their pastor.
The union was so great, I could not feel it my duty to give
a negative answer, although the pecuniary encouragement
appeared too small. I was ordained July 3, 1793, — a solemn
day to me. My deepest impression was, that I was insufficient for these things. I felt the force of that passage,
1 Kings, iii. 7, " I know not how to go out or come in before

the people." This was the subject of my first discourse after ordination.

Having been ordained about two years, I found the currency so much depreciated, that my salary was inadequate to my support. This was intimated to individuals, who circulated the report, that I could not continue with them much longer, unless some more pecuniary encouragement should be given. In consequence of this alarm, a universal disposition was shown to afford me voluntary assistance. From this encouragement I purchased a building spot, and about twenty acres of land entirely uncleared and unfenced. By the assistance of my parishioners, part of it was cleared up, and a house built, though unfinished. On Feb. 1, 1798, I was married to Rebecca Jones, the youngest daughter of John Jones, Esq., of Hopkinton. . . . After a long and distressing pulmonic consumption, she died March 2, 1811. She continued in the full exercise of her strong mental powers to the very last moment of life. I was married the second time, Nov. 12, 1812 | to Mary Jones Stimson |. She was the daughter of Doctor Jeremy Stimson [of Hopkinton], who married an elder sister of my former wife.

NOTE. — Mr. Clarke had nine children: viz., by his first wife, Abigail Morton Clarke, wife of the late John J. Stimson, of Providence, R.I.; William Pitt Clarke, of Ashland, Mass.: John Jones Clarke, of Roxbury, Mass.: Caroline Clarke, and George Leonard Clarke, both of whom died in infancy: by his second wife. George Leonard Clarke, of Providence, R.I.; Harriet Clarke, who died in infancy; Manlius Stimson Clarke, of Boston, who died in that city at the age of 37: and Edward Hammond Clarke, of Boston.

" HAVING prayerfully and diligently searched the Scriptures to obtain a knowledge of their truths, I present the following as the summary of my belief in the essential truths of the gospel." — *Rev. Pitt Clarke.*

CONFESSION OF FAITH;

OR,

A PASTOR'S LEGACY.

Jan. 1. 1835.

BRETHREN, — With the compliments of the season, I
present you a new year's gift, which is a small token
of my affection for you, and designed to imprint on your
mind a remembrance of me, your pastor. As I approach the
common age of man, I am moved to leave with you a written testimony of my earnest desire that you may all know
the truth, and be induced to walk in it. To aid your
endeavors, I send a printed copy of my views of religion
into all your families, entreating you to search the Scriptures
diligently, that you may see their conformity to the word of
God.

This I do for your good, and to satisfy the minds of some
who wish to know more fully my views of certain doctrines.

My preaching, say they, does not sufficiently discriminate between Trinitarianism and Unitarianism, Calvinism and Arminianism. I readily confess that I have not assumed either of these names, nor dwelt upon these sectarian points. In all these human creeds I find some good things, and some not supported in Scripture. The good I treasure up, the bad throw away. I profess to be a follower of Christ, and glory in being called a Christian, as his followers were first called Christians at Antioch. I have the example of my Master and his immediate followers, not to assume any name but Christian, — not to call any one master but Christ. Our Saviour was not a sectarian or an exclusionist, in the modern sense of these terms. Though he came to his own people and joined the Jewish Church, he made no attempt to proselyte to their peculiar faith. He was sent first to the lost sheep of the house of Israel; and he endeavored to convince them of dangerous errors, and also to enlighten all of every name, who would follow him as the Way, the Truth, and the Life. When his own people, who were set apart as holy unto the Lord, had become so exclusive as to have no dealings with the Samaritans on the ground of sentiment, he set up the Samaritan as the better man, and exhorted them to go and do likewise. Though I rank myself under no human leader, nor hold doctrines strictly called my own, — professing to believe only the doctrines of Christ, — nevertheless, I feel it highly important to have a firm belief in all the peculiar doctrines of the gospel, and am ready to declare openly what I receive as the doctrines of Christ, and as the faith once delivered to the saints.

I confess that *I cannot* believe in the peculiar doctrines of those called Trinitarians and Calvinists; for I cannot find them in any of our Saviour's preaching. His Sermon on the Mount, which contains the sum and the most important parts of his religion, says nothing about three co-equal persons in the Godhead, — nothing about the five points of Calvin. If it were important for us to believe these tenets, I am persuaded that our Saviour would have taught them. Instead of teaching any of these peculiarities, he clearly enforced doctrines of a different complexion. He made practical religion the groundwork of his system, saying to all who heard his words that they must *do* the will of their heavenly Father in order to find acceptance with him. He plainly taught that the doing of the will of God from the heart is the only way to build upon the right foundation. Instead of preaching the innate total depravity of little children, he took them into his arms as innocent subjects of his kingdom; and, when some forbade them, he said, " Forbid them not, for of such is the kingdom of heaven."

Respecting his union with the Father, he said no man knoweth who the Son is but the Father. The highest title he claimed was the Son of God, and he owned God to be his Father. He declared expressly that there is only one God, whom we are to worship, and him only to serve; that his mission was from heaven; that the works which he did bore witness that he came forth from God; and that he derived all his power and authority from the great Jehovah, who sanctified and sent him into the world, to do the will of his heavenly Father.

Having prayerfully and diligently searched the Scriptures to obtain a knowledge of their truths, I present the following as the summary of my belief in the essential truths of the gospel.

I believe that there is one only living and true God, the Father, of whom are all things, and we in him; and one Lord Jesus Christ, by whom are all things, and we by him.

I believe God to be an infinite Spirit, spreading the emanations of his being throughout the universe, possessing every adorable attribute and perfection. — the only proper object of supreme love, adoration, and praise. I believe him to be the Creator, Preserver, and Governor of the world; and that his government is perfectly just, wise, merciful, and good. I believe that he is continually within us and around us, extending his upholding power and superintending care to all beings and all worlds. I believe him to be the Giver of every good thing, the Source of all our blessings, and the righteous Judge of the world, before whom we must all appear to give up our final accounts.

I believe Jesus Christ to be the Son of God and Saviour of the world, possessing the same spirit with the Father. Paul says (Col. i. 15), "He is the first-born of every creature."

St. John says (Rev. iii. 14), "He is the beginning of the creation of God." I believe him to be the promised Messiah, and only Mediator between God and man. As a Mediator, I must view him as a distinct Being from the Father; for a mediator is one between two. If the Son be not a distinct Being from the Father, we have no Mediator nor Intercessor with God. For there is no other name given to be our Mediator but the Son. There is not the least intimation in prophecy that the Father would be the mediator between himself and man. A son was to be given, and the Son of God came in the fulness of time to be the Christ, the anointed of the Lord, to save his people from their sins. Jesus of Nazareth assumed this exalted character; and, when he was accused of blasphemy for it, he replied, "If those are called gods to whom the word of God came, sayest thou I blaspheme, because I call myself the Son of God?"

He is declared to be the Son of God with power, by his resurrection from the dead. If the Son be the same Being as the Father, then God must have died on the cross, and his death would have caused the destruction of the universe; for by him all things subsist. We all must and do make a distinction between the Father and the Son, when we view the latter as born of a virgin, nourished as a child, reasoning with the doctors, preaching among men, betrayed and crucified, lying dead in the grave, rising from the tomb. I believe all this was a *reality*, not a mere vision, an appearance of death and a resurrection. I believe that the Son of God actually suffered, died, and rose again; but the Father dwelt in him, raised him from the dead, and did, in and through him, all the wonderful works recorded of him in the Scriptures. I believe that in him the *word* was *made flesh;* i. e., that the *word* which was with God in the beginning of creation — the same as the energy of God speaking worlds into existence was in Christ when he took a human body — was thereby in the flesh, and dwelt among men. This word was in effect the same as God with us, and, by beholding its glory in Christ, we see the glory of the only begotten of the Father, full of grace and truth. But although God dwelt in his Son, and did the mighty works in him, still he gave the Son to have life in himself. This Jesus proved to the Jews, by making himself and his Father two distinct witnesses. He said, "I am one that bear witness of myself, and the Father beareth witness of me." If the Father and Son were one and the same Being, then Christ would have been a deceiver; for one Being could not be two witnesses.

I must therefore believe Christ to be only the Son of God, the brightness and the image of the invisible Jehovah, and that in him dwells the fulness of the Godhead bodily, and that through him we have access by one spirit unto the Father. Him hath God exalted to give repentance and remission of sin. By him we receive the atonement, even reconciliation with God; for in him, through him, or by him,

God is reconciling the world unto himself, not imputing unto men their trespasses.

I believe that God has given unto us eternal life, and that this life is in his Son in such a manner that all who yield obedience to his commands may enjoy it. I believe that God so loved the world as to manifest himself in flesh by Jesus Christ, who died and rose again, in order that life and immortality might be brought to light, that all mankind might be put into a state of salvation, and that every one might receive according to the deeds done in the body.

I believe that Christ came to make known the offers of salvation, and that he gave himself for us that he might redeem us from all iniquity, and purify us unto himself, a peculiar people, zealous of good works. I believe that he is able and willing to save all who come unto God by him, and that there is none other name under heaven given among men whereby we must be saved. I believe that God has exalted his Son to an equality with himself in the work of redemption, and given him a name above every name, that at the name of Jesus every knee should bow and every tongue confess him to be Lord, to the glory of God, the Father. By loving and honoring the Son, we love and honor the Father also. By receiving and walking with the Son, we receive and walk with the Father; for in both there is the same spirit, and they are co-workers in procuring the salvation of the soul. In this work, they are one; and Christ prayed that his followers might be one in the same spirit and temper, in the same design and pursuit. "Neither pray I for these alone, but for them also which shall believe on me through their word, that they all may be one, as thou, Father, art in me, and I in thee, that they also may be one in us, that the world may believe that thou hast sent me. And the glory which thou gavest me, I have given them, that they may be one, even as we are one" (John xvii. 20–22). In the same sense, he that planteth and he that watereth are one; and God giveth the increase.

I believe in the agency of the Holy Spirit, which is the spirit of God, working in the heart, convincing, restraining, and constraining; producing every thing that is good, giving efficacy to means in regeneration and conversion. I believe and baptize in the name of the Father, of the Son, and of the Holy Ghost: in devout acknowledgment of God, the Father of all; of Jesus Christ, the Son of God; and of the Holy Spirit, the inward Comforter and support of his people.

I believe in the necessity of a new birth, or a change of heart; for the natural birth gives no idea of God, or of eternity. That which is born of the flesh, is flesh, and sees and enjoys only fleshly gratifications. Children, though born innocent, are destitute of holiness, till they are capable of right affections. When the eyes of their mind are opened to see God and eternity, and the affections of their heart are placed on things above, then the new birth takes place. A new and spiritual world is opened to the view, the affections are raised from earthly to heavenly objects, and the whole man is brought into new and higher relations. I believe that this change of heart consists in a change of affections from sensual to spiritual enjoyments, from sin to holiness, from things seen and temporal to things unseen and eternal. If children grow up without any good instruction, or without setting their affections on things above as they are taught, and follow only the gratifications of the flesh, then, in order to enjoy God, they must become new creatures by putting off their old man, which is corrupt according to deceitful lusts, and by putting on the new man, which, after God, is created in righteousness and true holiness. I believe that this happy change is to be brought about through the instrumentality of God's word, blessed and sanctified by his Holy Spirit. We are born again, not of corruptible seed, but of incorruptible, by the word of God, which lives for ever. A Paul may plant, but God must give the increase.

I believe that this change is to be known by the fruits of it, which are good works. He who does righteousness is born of God. By this shall all men know that ye are my disciples, says Christ, if ye have love one to another. For love is the best evidence of a good heart. I do not believe in those conversions which make men more censorious and uncharitable. Genuine conversions make better hearts, tempers, and lives; better parents, children, neighbors, and citizens. Such conversions cause their subjects to become

more upright, humble, and peaceable; more charitable
towards those who differ in opinion; more willing to co-
operate with all good people in promoting practical piety.
I believe that sudden conversions are not so much to be
relied on as those more gradual, which have been brought
about by deliberate reflection and consideration; for the
subjects of sudden conversions may not know what spirit
they are of, till they have time to try the spirits, whether they
be of God. The fruits of a good spirit are love, joy, peace,
gentleness, humility, meekness, goodness, faith, hope, tem-
perance, &c.; the greatest of all, charity. I believe that
there are some good people in all denominations of Christians, and that, at the last day, a great multitude, which no
man can number, of all nations and kindreds and people
and tongues, will stand before the throne of God, clothed
with white robes, and palms of victory in their hands. I
believe that those who have no rule but the dim light of
nature are a law unto themselves, their consciences approv-
ing or disapproving of their conduct, and that they will be
judged accordingly.

But we who enjoy the Bible are bound to make this the
rule of our faith and practice; and by this book we shall be
finally judged. I believe that the final judgment will be in
perfect accordance with this grand principle of the gospel,
that God is no respecter of persons; but that in every nation
he that feareth him, and worketh righteousness, will be
accepted of him.

These are my views of that holy religion which is given
by the inspiration of God. I present them to you for your
perusal and assistance. It is my earnest prayer that you may
all receive them, and follow them, so far as they agree with
the sacred volume. They are designed to lead you to search
the Holy Scriptures more diligently, to examine the ground
of your faith more closely, to prove all things, and to hold
fast that which is good. I exhort you, not only to search the
Scriptures diligently and prayerfully, but to read them
connectedly. Much error arises from not comparing Scripture with Scripture. Different and apparently opposite
passages are to be compared together, and the more obscure
parts are to be explained by passages clearly understood.
I ask you to compare my views with Scripture, in this
connected sense. If, at first, you think that my views
differ from yours, and that you can find any passages of
Scripture against the leading articles of my faith, come as a
friend, and let me know it. I am willing to be judged by
the Bible; for I make this sacred volume the sole rule of
my faith, preaching, and practice. By this standard, we
must all be judged in the great day of accounts; and we
must receive according to the sentence which it shall then
give.

That you may not be deceived as to the foundation of
your faith and hope, it is of the utmost importance that you
lay aside all prejudice and wrong prepossessions, and let
the word of God have free course in your minds.

Finally, I add this exhortation, that you put away from among you all bitterness and malice and anger and evil speaking; and that ye be kind one to another, tender-hearted, forgiving one another in love, and that ye live in peace: then the God of love and peace will dwell with you.

POEMS

BY

MRS. MARY JONES CLARKE,

WITH AN

INTRODUCTORY SKETCH.

"Who hath not learned, in hours of faith,
   The truth to flesh and sense unknown,
   That Life is ever lord of Death,
   And Love can never lose its own?" — *Whittier.*

PREFACE.

THE annexed sketch of the life and character of Mrs. Clarke is substantially the same as that which appeared in the "Christian Register" for May 26, 1866. It was prepared by the Rev. Andrew Bigelow, D.D., whose acquaintance with her embraced a period of more than thirty years.

The Poems which follow the sketch are selected from Mrs. Clarke's manuscripts. They are her most fitting memorial. She was gifted with a fine poetic nature, and found her keenest enjoyment in poetic studies. She was familiar with the writings of the best English and American poets. When oppressed by care and anxiety, she would fly for refuge and relief to some favorite author. She was also fond of her pen, and composed with facility. Her deepest feelings, both of sorrow and joy, often found expression in poetry. She never intruded her writings upon the public. Only a few of them have been published. Her family and friends, however, often besieged her for a "piece of poetry;" a request to which she occasionally acceded. Most who knew her intimately will recognize the subjoined Poems as familiar friends. May they aid in keeping her memory fresh and green in the hearts of those who loved and cherished her!

E. H. C.

MEMOIR

OF

MARY JONES CLARKE.

MARY JONES CLARKE, second wife of Rev. Pitt Clarke, was the daughter of Dr. Jeremy Stimson, of Hopkinton, Mass. She was born in that place, March 24, 1785. She died in Providence, R.I., at the house of her son, George L. Clarke, Esq., May 1, 1866, at the advanced age of eighty-one years and two months.

The incidents in the life of Mrs. Clarke, beyond the ordinary experience of humanity, were few, and soon told. Married from a pleasant home, at a comparatively early period, to the pastor of a rural parish whose limits were co-extensive with the town, — a husband honorably known beyond its precincts, and in charge of youth from the University, claiming, aside from his parochial duties, special oversight and attention, — she accepted the requirements of the station, and met cheerfully the duties and responsibilities imposed. On the death of her husband, after upwards of twenty years of happy connubial fellowship, she removed to Cambridge, to be near and assist in the education of her two younger sons. Other youths in limited number, from the best families of the city, she consented to receive into her well-ordered household; and for fifteen years her dwelling was a blessed *appanage* of the University. In 1851, she moved to Boston, connecting herself with the Second Church in Bedford Street, under the care of Rev. Dr. Robbins. Thence, in 1856, she went to Dedham, making her home with an elder brother, Dr. Jeremy Stimson, of that place, still surviving to mourn a loss which other hearts unite to deplore. Two years later, Mrs. Clarke changed her residence for Providence, where, under the roof of a daughter peculiarly endeared, she passed the remainder of her days, until within a few weeks of her death, which occurred in the house of a son. But, during these years of apparent tranquillity and repose, the deceased was active. Her soul was ever alive, instinct with ardent solicitudes for the good of her fellow-kind. The churches with which she was severally connected have all known and felt the blessing of her labors. She was interested for the young. The Sunday school, as a potent instrumentality for their benefit, was an object near to her heart. She sought its improvement. To popularize its instructions, to induce and make pleasing to infantile minds its sacred influences and teachings, she turned into easy and familiar verse the many answers to the questions in the Channing Catechism for the young; a task (no effort to herself) so useful and approved, that it has been adopted and retained in divers of our sabbath schools, proving alike delightful and advantageous to the opening minds it was designed to reach. Mrs. Clarke, indeed, by taste and culture, had a refined and poetic mind. Some of her effusions, both in poetry and prose, have met the public eye, unheralded and untraced. She shrank from observation, glad to be useful or give pleasure from her quiet seclusion, content within the noiseless walks of life to remain unspoken of and unseen. Still she could not be hidden. All who approached her felt her influence. Of dignified aspect, keen, penetrating eye, benignant countenance, and tall, commanding person, none, first seeing her, could doubt the presence of no ordinary character. Yet there was nothing of *hauteur* in her bearing. She was gentle as a child. In her youth, she must have been handsome. We knew her first in the meridian, scarce past, — the bright meridian of her days. She was then the model woman; the model wife of a country clergyman: a model mother, sister, friend. Two years later, we met at the death-bed of the dearest object of her love. We were summoned, and went; and there at the midnight hour, wife, children, and their own " familiars " present, we wept, and kneeled and prayed. . . .

Mrs. Clarke, we need not say, was a Unitarian, intelligent, thoughtful, and devout. She early embraced the faith, believ-

ing in one God the Father, and his Son the only Mediator.
She looked to the cross, trusting to a dying, risen Lord; and,
having committed her soul to his keeping, moved steadfastly
on in the discharge of life's duties, and patient submission to
its trials, leaving the darkness of the present to be resolved
by the light of the future, and the shadowy and speculative
for the brightness and illumination alone to be had in a world
to come. She was eminently practical. Life to her was
earnest. The present was her sphere, labor her enjoyment
in the cause of truth and right; and, for other recompense,
she looked to the "glory to be revealed." Her sympathies
were large, embracing the poor and outcast, the friend-
less and suffering of every shade and name. The wrongs
of the slave were an object of her thoughtful solicitudes.
By pen and word (none more eloquent) she wrought
for his emancipation. Years ago, in the darkest hours
of his bondage, she predicted its sure and no distant
accomplishment. She lived to see the fulfilment, though
in ways she thought not of. For she believed in God, and
that the "Judge of the whole earth would do that which is
right."

Wide and warm as were her sympathies, her affections in
the domestic and closer relations of life could not fail to be
tenderer and more strong. Her family loves were recipro-
cated with a warmth and fervor seldom surpassed; and in
the less restricted circle of intimates she was held in admir-
ing and exalted estimation.

Her latter end was peace. It could not be otherwise. The final limit was reached by a gradual and protracted decline. Her exit was serene, painless the close.

> " Not night-dews fall more gently to the ground.
> Nor weary, worn-out winds expire so soft.

"Nor mourn, O Living One! because
Her part in life was mourning.
Would she have lost the poet's fire,
For anguish of the burning?" — *Mrs. Browning.*

POEMS.

HYMN

Written for the Dedication of a Church in Norton.

—•—

O THOU whose eye all space surveys,
　　Who every heart canst read,
Each dark disguise canst pierce, and see
　　The motive in the deed!
Here we in holy awe would stand,
　　From earthly passions free:
" While, in the confidence of prayer,
　　Our souls take hold on thee."

This earthly temple, made with hands,
　　To thee we set apart,
And here in faith and hope would yield
　　The offering of the heart.

7

Nor would we, Lord, while thee we praise,
  In solemn mockery kneel:
The daily mercies we receive,
  Give us the heart to feel.

Here may the soul, though drawn to earth,
  And chained by thousand ties, —
Here may she break her worldly bonds!
  Here may she learn to rise!
Thine aid impart, when, fierce and strong,
  Temptations dark assail:
O God! our wavering purpose fix,
  When better thoughts prevail.

Oh! glorious is our Father's house,
  With many mansions fair;
Nor ear hath heard, nor eye hath seen,
  The glories we may share.
But strait the path that thither leads,
  And narrow is the way;
Unnumbered snares are round us spread:
  Lord, save us, or we stray.

H Y M N.

Sunset in Summer.

—◆—

H OW gloriously the setting sun
    Sinks to his evening rest,
And hides his glowing face beneath
    The crimson-curtained west!

How beautiful the wandering cloud,
    When the long day is done;
The bright, the brilliant canopy,
    That waits the setting sun!

The breeze is softly blowing
    The perfume from the tree,
And beauty spreads her magic tints
    O'er all the eye can see.

'Tis glory, happiness, and peace,
　　Where God has given the power,
'To feel the influence, and bless
　　The beauty of the hour.

LINES

Occasioned by reading Mr. Peabody's Discourses on the Death of his Wife and Daughter.

B LESSINGS, may countless blessings rest
On that pure heart of thine,
For pouring o'er life's darkest scenes
Those rays of light divine!
When thy sad heart was breaking,
In sorrow's darkest hour,
Deep in thy soul a spirit waked
Sources of unknown power.

When even heart and hope had failed,
On every side distressed,
"Thy soul was resolute and still,
And calm and self-possessed."

The holy peace that through thy breast
In silent rapture steals,
A heavenly radiance pours around,
A mighty hope reveals.

SUNSET AND EVENING IN SUMMER.

•—

OH! tell not of Italian skies,
　　Nor of her sunny bowers:
No land, where brooks or rivers run,
Can show at eve a fairer sun
　　Or lovelier skies than ours.

How soft above the crimson cloud
　　The changing splendors fly,
And bear a train of glory bright
　　Far up the western sky!
A fairer sight was never seen
　　By any human eye.

And when, in tranquil beauty,
　　The evening stars come forth,

And climbs upon the upper air
   The enchantress of the north,
How deep the spell that binds us!
   The scene, how passing fair!
Those waving, shadowy streams of light
Now dazzle and now cheat the sight,
And seem, like spirits of the night,
   To join in gambols there.

The living light of other spheres
   Beams on the lifted eye:
Ten thousand wonders are revealed,
Ten thousand wonders are concealed,
   In ocean, earth, and sky.

Surely they err who tell us
   That this fair world of ours
Is evil, evil only,
   When God has given us powers
To see the beautiful and good,
   And taste the heavenly bliss
That pours its treasures o'er the soul,
   On such a night as this.

In such an hour, no low desires,
   No earth-born wishes, rise;

The soul, all conscious of her powers,
   Claims kindred with the skies.
She feels immortal hopes expand,
   Sees unknown glories shine,
Her native dignity asserts,
   And knows she is divine.

THE SUMMER SHOWER.

HOW dark is yon cloud that rolls up from the west!
   How brilliant the flashes that gleam from his crest!
How threatening his aspect, and dreadful the glare,
As if ruin and death and destruction were there!
Now loud and still louder he comes on his way,
With the darkness of night and the brightness of day;
And, trembling, we shrink from the glance of his eye,
As the giant in grandeur and terror goes by.
But soon he has passed, and dispersed are our fears:
The sun in the strength of his glory appears;
While lovely and graceful, the beautiful bow
Bends o'er his dark front with her radiant glow.
How pure and unmixed is the beautiful blue!
The rose has assumed a still lovelier hue;
How fresh are the flowers, how fragrant the air!
What scene more delightful, what prospect more fair?
And say, such a scene can you purchase with wealth?
Oh! 'tis freshness and vigor and beauty and health.

THE RETURN.

Written after her Husband's Funeral.

◆—

WE came where the footsteps of death had been,
   And he seemed to linger near,
His breath o'er the home of affection had passed,
O'er the silent room, the deserted hearth,
   And chilled the atmosphere.

We listened for the well-known step,
   The well-known voice to hear;
We looked in vain when the board was spread,
   And at the hour of prayer;
And in the house of worship, too,
   There was a stranger there.

And now, when night is closing in,
   And cold winds whistle drear,

Where is that strong, sustaining arm,
  That all-providing care?
Alas! alas! the aching heart!
  It whispers of despair.

Should want invade, should grief oppress,
Should sickness, care, and wretchedness
  Steal o'er his much-loved home,
His hand no more averts the ill;
Our joy or sorrow, woe or weal,
  Alike to him unknown.

And days shall come, and years pass by,
And not a sorrow or a sigh
  Disturb his endless sleep;
" And not a care shall dare intrude,
To break the marble solitude,
  So peaceful and so deep."

And yet there is a brighter view,
Where better, holier feelings dwell;
And I can hear a secret voice
Whisper my soul, that all is well.

TO A SON IN COLLEGE.

- ◆ -

LIKE a young courser bounding o'er the plain,
   Strength in each nerve, and health in every vein,
I see thee start in life's eventful race,
Fresh for the field and eager for the chase.
Yet pause: not always does the race belong
Unto the swift, or battle to the strong.
A thousand pitfalls may thy steps betray;
A thousand unseen dangers throng thy way.
Life's evils all untried, — how canst thou know
The countless ills that on its current flow?
And youth is heedless of its mines of wealth;
Its ample store of talents, strength, and health;
And golden opportunities, that rise
To make it useful, happy, good, and wise.
Fearless of danger, confident and bold,
Not half the ills that throng thee can be told.

Oh! then, beware, reason and conscience hear;
The "still small voice" of God within revere;
Or lost to virtue, lost to health and fame,
You fall where many mightier have been slain.

A PRAYER.

GOD of the good and happy, hear my prayer,
And take my much-loved children to thy care.
Save them from sin and suffering: let me still
Have power to shield and shelter them from ill;
To make fair virtue's path attractive seem,
Teach them that youth is passing like a dream;
And early fix their views on that bright shore.
Where sin and sorrow shall invade no more.

THANKSGIVING OFFERING.

Written for a Family Gathering.

WE'LL leave awhile life's wasting cares,
   Its sorrows, toil, and strife,
For love, the sweetest flower that blooms
   Upon the tree of life,
The treasure of the infant's heart,
   Youth's most delicious dream,
The crown of manhood, joy of age,
   Its brightest, holiest beam.

O Love and Hope, bright beings sent
   To cheer our path below!
What were this world without your light,
   Or that to which we go?
Assembled at affection's call,
   United heart and hand,
Thy blessing, Father, we implore
   On this, our little band.

The widow and the fatherless,
  The mother and the child,
Manhood mature, and thoughtless youth,
  And childhood laughing wild,
All gathered round the festive board,
  Their various offerings pour,
And bless thee for the mercies past,
  And for the joys in store.

Bright hopes — a never-fading wreath —
  And cheerful hearts we bring,
And learn, at length, our dearest joys
  May from our sorrows spring.
Watered with tears, the tree of life
  Bursts into sudden bloom;
Part of the fruit matures on earth,
  And part beyond the tomb.

But one is missing from our side
  Whose smile could always cheer;
We miss him, as the summer flower
Misses the sunshine and the shower:
  Oh, would that he were here!
And one, a darling little one,
  The youngest of our band,
Since last we met, a home has found
  Far in the spirit land.

Though, thickly scattered o'er our path,
Sorrows and cares are strown, —
Thanks be to God! life's deepest woes
Our souls have never known.
What though our days glide swiftly by,
And life has ills untold,
We'll keep our feelings fresh and warm,
Nor let our hearts grow old.

THOUGHTS OF THE LOVED AND LOST.

ONCE I had hoped, — that hope how vain! —
    Had hoped to see thee stand,
Honored and loved, amongst the good
    And gifted of the land.

How strangely sad all things appear!
    Where shall I seek relief?
The very atmosphere I breathe
    Seems heavy now with grief.

Far on life's outward boundary,
    With beating heart I stand:
Behind me lies a desert waste;
    Before, an unknown land.

Dark clouds are gathering round my path,
  Death shadows flitting by;
While voices from the spirit world
  Seem calling me on high.

Not here thy rest, they seem to say;
  Oh! seek not here for bliss:
The soul's true rest cannot be found
  In such a world as this.

I'm sick at heart and weary;
  My spirit sighs for rest,
To be where happy beings dwell, —
  A blest one with the blest.

WANT OF SYMPATHY.

♦ —

OH! did they know the magic power
   Kind looks and words impart,
Know all the power to bless that lies
   In every human heart, —

One-half the ills that bind us down
   With such a heavy chain
Would be unfelt, and of the rest
   We little should complain.

Our pain would almost turn to bliss,
   To joy our sorrow turn,
And we, though suffering and distrest,
   Almost forget to mourn.

Take sunshine from the flower,
　Take blossoms from the tree, —
Where its fragrance, where its fruit,
　Where will its beauty, be?

Even such is woman's heart, —
　A drooping, blasted thing, —
Without the sunshine of a smile,
　And love's protecting wing.

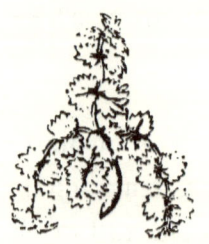

DESPONDENCY.

—

THROUGH this sad, varying scene of life,
  Of weariness and pain,
Where some bright glimpses meet the eye,
  Then all is dark again:

Through sorrows that have passed away,
  But left their sting behind;
O'er blighted hopes and buried joys. —
  My weary way I wind.

The flowers will never bloom as sweet,
  Birds never sing again,
As when, in early, happier days,
  I listened to their strain.

My heart is like a broken harp,
   A tuneless, ruined thing,
Though sometimes music, sad and sweet,
   May from the ruin spring,
Drawn forth by some mysterious power,
Some wandering spirit of the hour,
   That strikes the secret string.

THE DINNER.

A PUZZLE.

Addressed to the Brother of the Authoress.

—◆—

A S a number intend to-morrow
  To dine
With you and your lady, they thought
  That a line
Might not be improper, that you
  May prepare
Whatever you choose, that is costly
  And rare.

 · · · · · · ·

And first, then, in order, your father
  And mother,
And with them will come your sister
  And brother;

Your great-uncle also, if he shall
      See fit,
And his goodly old dame, if her health
      Will admit.
Your cousin Maria, too, means
      To be there,
With her lively young husband ; a gay
      Youthful pair.
Your uncle and aunt, too, if they can
      Crowd in,
To join in the party will think it
      No sin.
And they trust, after taking such labor
      And pain,
To taste your Madeira, if not your
      Champagne.

          .   .   .   .   .   .

The company came; all the party
      Were there, —
Stop a moment, I'll tell you how many
      There were.
When all had been counted, — aunts, uncles,
      And cousin, —
Add ten to the number, you'll have just
      A dozen.

TO MY SPECTACLES.

＊—

I DO not covet such a friend as thou,
  To ornament the precincts of my brow;
Nor does my nose feel thankful for thy weight:
Indeed, thy sight and feeling, too, I hate.
Sitting astride upon thy gristly throne,
Thou seem'st upon my sufferings to look down
With thy large glassy eyes, and to make known
That they are now more useful than my own.
Besides, thou never canst a secret keep,
But plainly say'st to all that I am old;
And, tell-tale like, the story wilt repeat
To every being thou dost e'er behold.

FORTY-EIGHT.

A T sober, honest forty-eight,
    I pause upon my way,
And stop to look around awhile,
    And see how goes the day.

"Indeed," says Time, "that will not do:
    You shall not stop nor stay:
The clouds are dark, the wind is high,
And yonder hill your strength will try;
    So speed thee on thy way."

"But Time, old Time, I wish to stop,
    And breathe a little space;
Besides, I want to look behind,
And see how many I can find
    That started in the race.

Thy cruel hand hath swept away
  So many friends of mine.
That I would closer draw around
The very few that can be found.
  Nor all to thee resign.

My youthful hopes, my early friends,
  My better days, are fled;
And now pray tell me what it is
  Thou hast given me instead.

My eyes are dim, my ear is dull,
  My hair is turning gray;
And memory, like a summer friend.
  Now steals so fast away,
That I scarce ever can believe
  A word that she may say."

" Hush, hush," says Time, " we'll reckon soon;
  And, when I pay my score,
None e'er were known, or to complain,
  Or ever ask for more."

THE LITTLE BOY'S SONG.

—◆—

OH! 'tis a lovely evening:
    How bright the deep blue sky!
And thick the blossoms from the trees
    Come gently floating by.

The air is rich in fragrance;
    The earth, in beauty fair;
While, sparkling in their distant homes,
    Unnumbered worlds appear.

I wish they would come nearer,
    That I might take a peep
At all the wonders that are hid
    In the distant, dark-blue deep.

I love a summer evening,
  So calm, so fair, so bright;
The cool and pleasant breezes,
  The moonbeam's silver light.

I love to look upon the sky,
  On a splendid night in June;
To listen to the whippoorwill,
  And gaze upon the moon.

And when, as summer wears away,
  And her brighter tints are hid,
I love to hear the August fly,
  And the noisy katydid.

I sometimes think that voices
  Are singing in the air;
And, if I had a pair of wings,
  I'd very soon be there.

Oh! youth's a happy season,
  If rightly understood;
And I am very sure that none
  Are happy but the good.

HEALTH AND INDOLENCE AT THE BEDSIDE
OF A LADY.

— ✦ —

INDOLENCE.

O GENTLE lady! rise not yet:
    The morning air is cold,
And lovely visions o'er your head
    Shall wave their wings of gold.

Your bed of down, how soft and warm!
    Sweet slumbers seal your eyes;
No fears disturb, no cares molest:
    Then, lady, do not rise.

Sleep, till the sun, with silent pace,
    Has reached his highest noon;
Then rise to breathe the fragrant breath,
    And balmy air of June.

H E A L T H.

O lady! list not to the lay
  That artful siren sings:
No tongue the countless woes can tell
  That in her train she brings.

Then, lady, rise: the morning air
  Your languid frame shall brace:
Shall give new vigor to your step,
  And beauty to your face.

The eastern skies are tinged with gold;
  Rich music fills the air;
There's perfume on the morning breeze,
  And beauty everywhere.

Oh! waste not thus the morning's prime,
  Nor let me call in vain;
Think, lady, think: if now refused,
  I ne'er may call again.

.   .   .   .   .

The lady heard the warning voice;
  Her heart was filled with dread;
Her curtain slowly she unclosed,
  And raised her languid head.

11

With anxious eye she gazed around,
Then tried in vain to rise;
While Indolence, with gentle force,
Pressed down her weary eyes.

With charms invisible, though strong.
She kept her in her power;
Nor was that lady seen again
In garden, hall, or bower.

THE GOLD AND SILVER TREE OF SLAVERY.

— ✦ —

[It appears from the date affixed to the following verses, that they were written in 1840. This fact, when we consider the history of the last few years, gives an added interest to the poem. Mrs. Clarke lived to see the literal fulfilment of the prophecy with which the poem closes.]

COME, all who human rights revere;
    Come, all ye brave and free;
And let us gaze awhile upon
    This gold and silver tree.

Its trunk of polished silver seemed;
    Its branches, bright and fair,
Stretched far and wide their giant arms,
    That glittered in the air.

Around its head bright rainbow hues
  In circling glory rolled:
The blossoms all were diamonds bright,
  And all the leaves were gold.

The sap that fed this silver tree,
  And through its branches strayed,
Was not from nature's fountains drawn,
  In nature's storehouse made.

Oh, no! 'twas quite another thing
  That nourished every part:
'Twas blood from human bosoms drawn,
  Fresh from the beating heart.

In blood its roots were steeped, and blood
  In secret flowed around;
While clustering leaves concealed the fruit
  That on this tree was found.

The breeze that waved its brilliant leaves
  Was formed of human sighs;
The showers that o'er its blossoms fell
  Were tears from human eyes.

Come, all who hope for better days:
    Come, all ye good and free:
And let us see the fruit that grows
    Upon this silver tree.

It bore a talisman of power
    To turn all wrong to right:
'Twas right to rob, 'twas right to steal.
    To murder, and to fight.

'Twas right to sever nature's ties,
    So strong and holy made;
The mother from the child to tear,
    The human soul degrade: —

To sell a man, with heart and head,
    A body and a soul, —
To sell him like a common thing,
    God's image sell, for gold.

Yet see, this golden Upas tree
    Still wide and wider spreads,
And over all the sunny South
    Its deadly venom sheds.

Wider and wider still it spreads,
　Though rotten to the core;
And deeper still its roots extend,
　Though steeped in human gore.

How, for the South, the blood-stained South,
　For this her guilt and shame!
She sowed broadcast the seeds of woe,
　And she must reap the same.

Shrouded in mystery and gloom,
　Scarce seen his threatening eye,
The genius of the future came,
　And raised his standard high.

And written on his blood-red flag
　Was seen, while waving slow,
" Oceans of blood have nursed this tree,
　And blood for blood must flow."

JOSEPHINE

Signing the Articles of Separation from Napoleon.

— ◆ —

IN silent majesty she stood,
  The shadow of a queen:
How many hearts shall bleed for thee,
  Imperial Josephine!

And he, thy loved and haughty lord, —
  Why sinks he not in earth,
To lay on low ambition's shrine
  This pearl of priceless worth?

No loud reproach, no bitter words,
  The soul's deep anguish speak:
Though fast and silently the tears
  Flow down thy pallid cheek.

. . .

'Twas not because the diadem
  Was passing from thy brow:
'Twas not because the fickle crowd
  Would to thy rival bow: —

Oh, no! 'twas woman's trusting heart,
  That must its hopes resign,
That forced the life-blood from thy cheek,
  Thou peerless Josephine.

A glory circles round thy brow,
  By true hearts understood;
Not that a throne was thine, but thou
  Wast faithful, tried, and good.

While thus I mused with aching heart,
  On sorrows such as thine,
I heard a gentle spirit sing
  This requiem at thy shrine: —

O woman, formed to suffer every ill,
For lordly man to triumph o'er at will:
To see her hoard of rich affections lost,
Or trifled with as things of little cost!
Cherish, as Heaven's best gift, the yielding mind,
That bears and hopes and weeps and is resigned.

Oh! happy, doubly happy, 'tis for thee,
Thy Maker formed thee like the willow-tree,
That bends its head beneath the tempest's blast,
And shrinking, bending, yielding, to the last,
Feels all the tempest's wrath; and, when 'tis o'er,
Spreads its green leaves to catch the breeze once more.

736961 A

THE OAK AND THE WILLOW.

A FABLE.

U PON a green hill's sloping side,
   An oak his arms outspread:
Divided from the neighboring wood,
Alone in silent strength he stood,
   A solitary shade.
Full fifty winters o'er his head
   Had poured their snow and sleet;
Full fifty summers' scorching suns
   Upon his head had beat.
And summer's heat, and winter's cold,
   His trunk but firmer made;
In vain the tempest o'er him past,
Along his boughs the northern blast
   All innocently played.

Within the circle of his shade,
  By chance a willow grew:
She was a lonely little thing,
And, watered by a neighboring spring,
  Unnoticed rose to view.
The birds that sung beneath her shade,
The breeze that through her branches played,
  Were all the friends she knew.

But days passed on: the willow now
  A graceful height had gained,
And to the wandering breezes gave
  Her branches unrestrained.
But oft her head beneath the blast
  Was bent so deep and low,
That scarcely could her trunk sustain,
And scarce her branches could again
  Recover from the blow.

The oak had marked her youthful form,
  Her unprotected state:
And thought, in silence as he gazed,
  To take her for his mate.
While thus revolving in his heart
  How best his suit to gain,
Sudden a tempest rose, and swept
  Across the neighboring plain.

The oak his giant arms outspread,
And, high above the willow's head,
   The tempest's shock sustained.
The storm passed on, and sunshine now
   And zephyrs round them played;
When, smoothing down his rugged points,
   His suit he thus essayed: —

"Come, gentle one, and dwell with me,
And my strong arms shall shelter thee,
   And guard from every ill;
Nor winter's cold shall do thee harm,
Nor summer's heat nor furious storm
   Thy peace shall e'er invade."

The willow heard his song of love,
   And raised her drooping head;
But what she thought I may not tell,
   Nor tell you what she said.
But soon their branches they unite,
   An intermingled shade.

And Time passed on: for never yet
   For mortal wight he stayed;
Nor of his speed will aught abate,
   Though oaks and willows wed.

One day, as Zephyr passed, he heard
  The willow thus complain:
"True, I've protection got; but then
  At what a price 'tis gained!
True, when alone, I often thought
  No one my sorrow heeds;
But now, by rough collision torn,
  This bosom always bleeds."

If for support she twined around
  His branches, sharp and strong;
Or only by the playful breeze
  Her arms were round him thrown, —
Which way soe'er she turned her head,
  Encountered still a thorn.
For, hard and bare, his rugged arms
  Now harder still were grown;
And time had crusted o'er his form
  With roughness once unknown.
No longer now with branches free,
  And waving in the wind;
No longer now, in living green,
  Her fading form we find:
But torn and battered are her boughs;
  Her glory all has passed;
And o'er her broken, withered form
  Decay is stealing fast.

Zephyr, who never sorrow knew,
　Nor ever tarried long,
One moment listened as he passed,
　Then gave this parting song: —

" Good Mrs. Oak, if you content
　Miss Willow had remained,
You had not met with this mishap,
　Nor this disgrace sustained.

The oak with other oaks should mate;
　With elms, the elm should wed;
The willow, by the running brook,
　Should droop her pensive head,
And, o'er the violet-covered bank
　In graceful ease reclined,
Should twine her green and pliant boughs
　With others of her kind.
Think not, when thus the very laws
　Of nature you have broke,
That bliss the union can attend
　Of the willow and the oak."

www.ingramcontent.com/pod-product-compliance
Lightning Source LLC
Chambersburg PA
CBHW020038030726
47499CB00007B/2493